A Letter
To Granny

Paul Rogers · John Prater

The Bodley Head

London

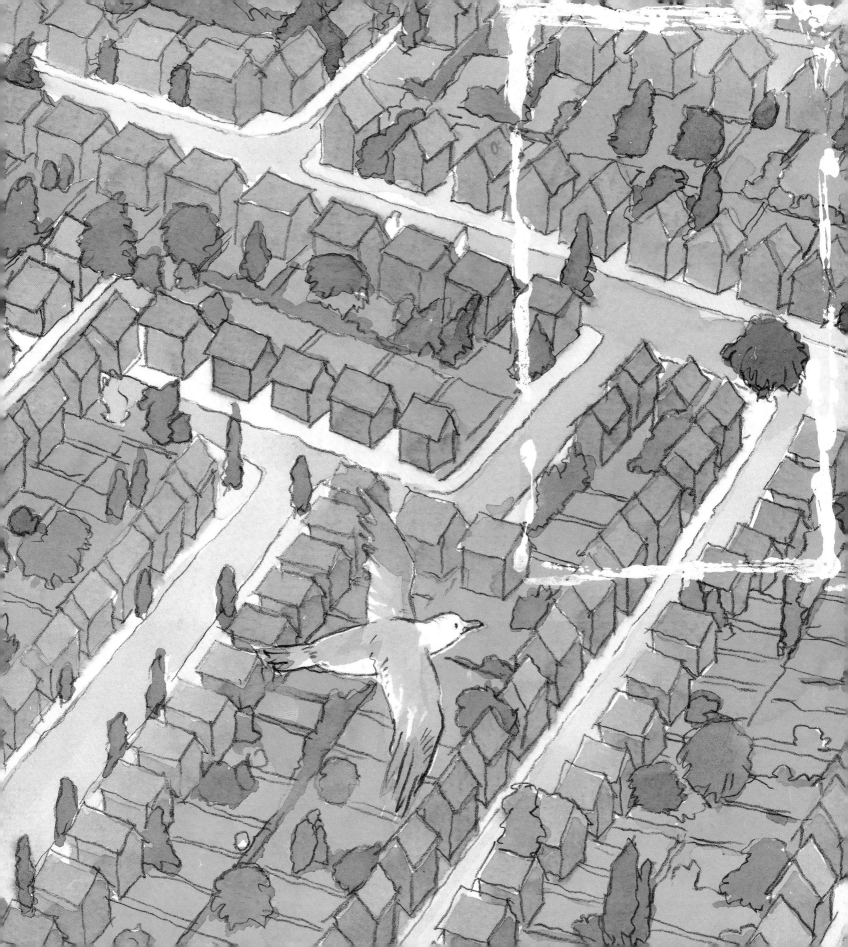

For Laura and Clara – PR

1 3 5 7 9 10 8 6 4 2

Copyright © text Paul Rogers 1994
Copyright © illustrations John Prater 1994

Paul Rogers and John Prater have asserted their rights under the
Copyright, Designs and Patents Act, 1988 to be identified as the
author and illustrator of this work

First published in the United Kingdom 1994
by The Bodley Head Children's Books
Random House, 20 Vauxhall Bridge Road, London SW1 2SA

Random House Australia (Pty) Limited
20 Alfred Street, Milsons Point, Sydney,
New South Wales 2061, Australia

Random House New Zealand Limited
18 Poland Road, Glenfield,
Auckland 10, New Zealand

Random House South Africa (Pty) Limited
PO Box 337, Bergvlei 2012, South Africa

Random House UK Limited Reg. No. 954009

A CIP catalogue record for this book is available from the
British Library

ISBN 0 37 031878 1

Printed in Hong Kong

Lucy lay in her bed, in her room, in her house, in her street, and thought of the whole town spread out around her.

She fell asleep listening to night noises – distant cars and dogs barking into the dark – and thinking about tomorrow, when Granny would come.

The moment she woke, she knew
something was different. Where had all
the houses gone? The streets? The town?
From her window she could see nothing
but sea!

She ran out of the house, barefoot
on to the sand – past the garden,
past the garage, past the front door, under
her own bedroom window.

'Breakfast's ready!' Mum called.

Lucy climbed back up the cliff, leaving
a necklace of footprints around the island.

'The postman's late,' said Dad.

'I expect the traffic's bad,' said Mum.

'I'm going out to watch the whales,'
said Lucy.

That's where my school used to be, she thought, over there. This is where the road was. She picked up a starfish. 'And there,' she laughed, as two crabs scuttled away, 'that's where Mr and Mrs Horner lived.'

At lunchtime, Lucy told Mum and Dad all about the rock pools, the fish and the sea. But they didn't seem to be listening.

During pudding there was a knock at the door.
'I'll go!' Lucy said.

An enormous liner was anchored off the front garden. On the step stood its captain. 'Pardon me,' he said. 'I think we're lost. I can't work out where I am.'

'This is 101 Acacia Road,' said Lucy.

'Ah, thank you,' said the captain. 'Sorry to trouble you.'

After lunch Lucy's parents worked in the garden.
'Look at these lupins!' complained Mum.

'Look at those dolphins!' called Lucy from the beach.

Suddenly she remembered Granny.
How ever would she get here now?
Someone would have to tell her!
At her toes Lucy saw an old bottle.
She hurried indoors for pen and
paper and wrote:

Dear Granny,
I can't wait to see you.
Our new address is
101 Acacia Road Island.
Please come soon.
Love from Lucy

Then rolling the message up, she
slipped it into the bottle and pushed
it out to sea.

That was when Lucy felt the first drops of rain. The sky grew dark, the sea grew wild, and soon Lucy was hurrying to the house for shelter. From the window she watched the storm.

Now Granny will never make it, she thought.

Then, way out in the distance, she spotted a small boat. One moment it was riding a giant wave, the next it was lost from sight. But gradually it grew bigger and bigger until Lucy could make out her Granny, waving.

'Hello Granny!' she called, running to the water's edge as the rain stopped. Together they climbed the path to the house.

'You look a bit wet,' said Dad. 'Did you have to wait for the bus?'

After tea, Lucy took Granny on a tour of the island. She showed her the crabs and gulls, the rock pools and starfish.

'Look,' said Granny, 'I've something for you. Hold it to your ear. What do you hear?'

So Lucy pressed the warm-coloured, soft-looking, cold, hard shell to her ear. And in it she heard the sound of the sea.

Then she sat on Granny's lap, on the deckchair, on the beach, on the island, and together they watched the ripe sun going down.

When it was time for Granny to go, Lucy waved her goodbye from the gate. She watched her climbing into the boat and sailing slowly, slowly away.

'Time for bed,' said Dad.

'I expect Granny will steer by the stars,' said Lucy.

That night, Lucy fell asleep listening to the
sighing of the sea and dreaming all about . . .

. . . tomorrow.

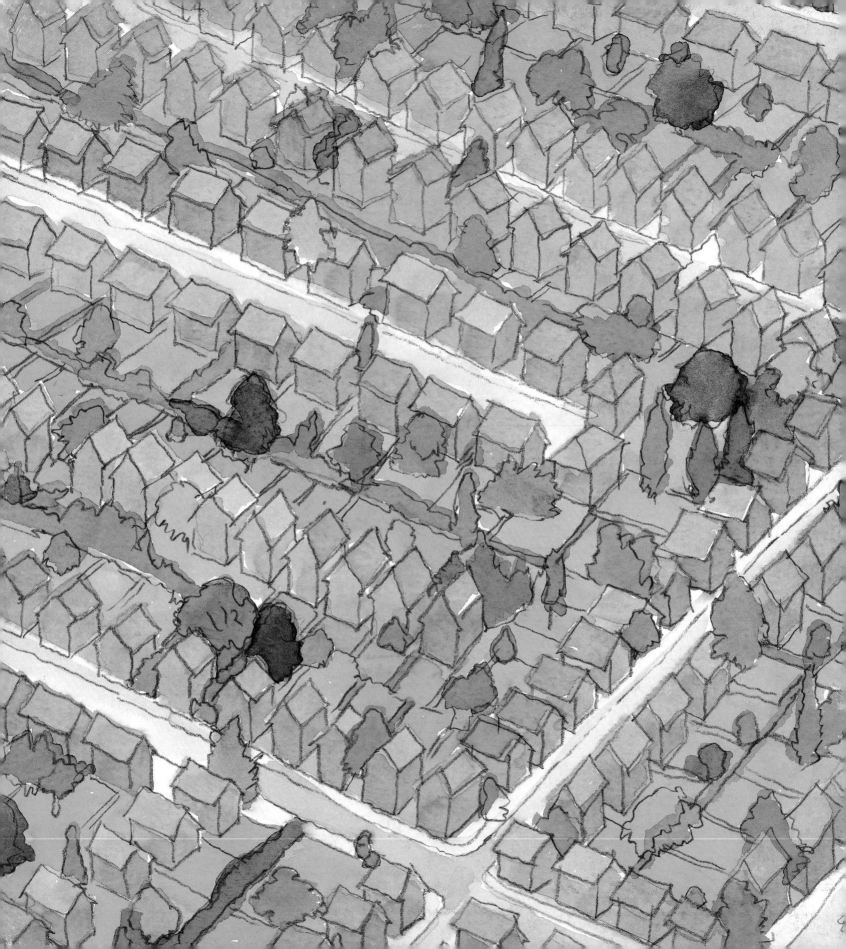